TRICYCLE PRESS • BERKELEY, CALIFORNIA

Remy Charlip
ARM IN ARM

*A COLLECTION
OF CONNECTIONS
ENDLESS TALES
REITERATIONS
AND OTHER ECHOLALIA*

LIBRARY OF CONGRESS
CATALOGING-IN-PUBLICATION DATA

CHARLIP, REMY.
ARM IN ARM: A COLLECTION OF CONNECTIONS,
ENDLESS TALES, REITERATIONS,
AND OTHER ECHOLALIA / REMY CHARLIP.
P. CM.
SUMMARY: AN ILLUSTRATED COLLECTION
OF VERSES, TONGUE TWISTERS, RIDDLES,
AND ENDLESS TALES ALL OF WHICH
FEATURE A PLAY ON WORDS AND IMAGES.
ISBN 1-883672-50-3
[1. PLAY ON WORDS—JUVENILE
LITERATURE.] I. TITLE
P304.C47   1997
808.87—DC21   96-44370
CIP
AC

TRICYCLE PRESS
P.O. BOX 7123
BERKELEY, CALIFORNIA 94707
ORIGINALLY PUBLISHED BY PARENTS' MAGAZINE PRESS, 1969
FIRST TRICYCLE PRESS PRINTING, 1997
PRINTED IN SINGAPORE
1 2 3 4 5 6
97 98 99 00 01

THIS BOOK IS DEDICATED TO MARIA IRENE FORNÉS

TWO OCTOPUSES GOT MARRIED AND WALKED DOWN THE AISLE ARM IN ARM IN ARM IN ARM IN ARM IN ARM IN ARM IN ARM IN ARM IN ARM IN ARM IN ARM IN ARM IN ARM IN ARM IN ARM.

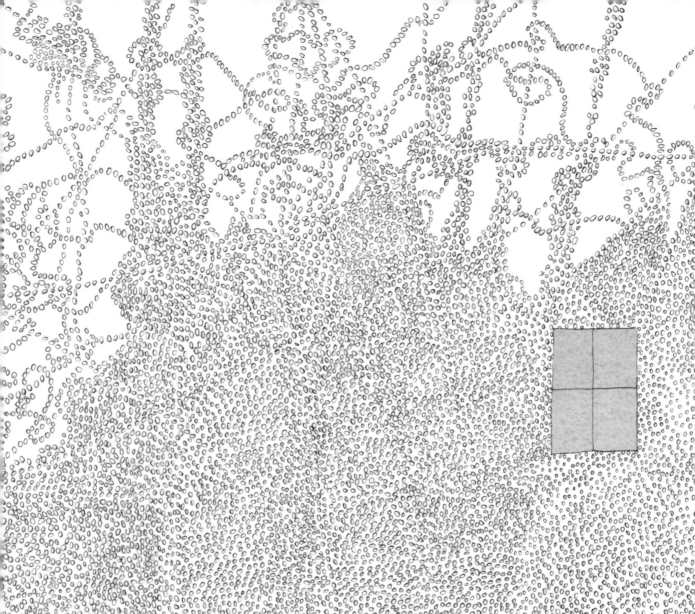

ISN'T IT BETTER TO BE OUT IN THE COLD
SNOW SAYING, "ISN'T IT BETTER TO BE OUT
IN THE COLD SNOW RATHER THAN IN A WARM
BED?" RATHER THAN IN A WARM BED SAYING,
"ISN'T IT BETTER TO BE OUT IN THE COLD
SNOW RATHER THAN IN A WARM BED?"

IT WAS A DARK AND STORMY NIGHT. WE WERE STANDING ON THE DECK. THE SHIP WAS SINKING. THE CAPTAIN SAID TO ME: "TELL ME A STORY, MY SON." AND SO I BEGAN: "IT WAS A DARK AND STORMY NIGHT. WE WERE STANDING ON THE DECK. THE SHIP WAS SINKING. THE CAPTAIN SAID TO ME: 'TELL ME A STORY, MY SON.' AND SO I BEGAN, 'IT WAS A DARK AND STORMY NIGHT. WE WERE STANDING ON THE DECK...'"

NO WORM
NO BIRD
NO CAT
NO DOG
NO PERSON
NO HOUSE
NO TREE
NO WOODS
NO LAND
NO WATER
NO CLOUDS
NO SKY
NO SUN
NOTHING

NO PICTURE

HOW THEATER WAS BORN

A PLAY

FIRST CAVEMAN: (HITTING SECOND CAVEMAN WITH CLUB) UGH! WHACK!
SECOND CAVEMAN: (PASSING OUT) OUCH!
CAVEBOY: (APPLAUDING) HOORAY! HOORAY! DO IT AGAIN.

WHAT IS WRITTEN ON THE OTHER SIDE OF THIS PAGE IS WRONG.

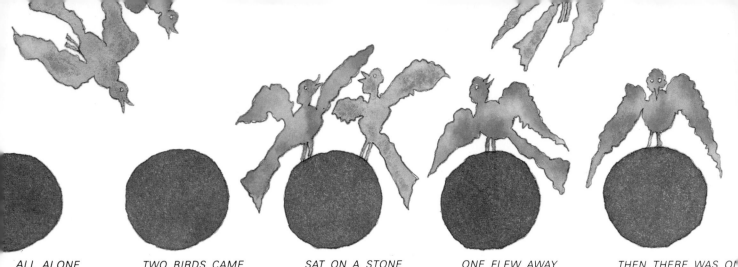

ALL ALONE   TWO BIRDS CAME   SAT ON A STONE   ONE FLEW AWAY   THEN THERE WAS O

MY SONG IS NOT LONG

THE OTHER FLEW AWAY THEN THERE WAS NONE POOR STONE ALL ALONE TWO BIRDS CAME SAT ON A STONE

WHO WAS FIRST ME OR YOU?

DON'T QUESTION IT, BE GRATEFUL WE HAVE ONE ANOTHER

 AN OCTOPUSS

THE FAIRY'S WISH

A PLAY

(FAIRY ENTERS TO GRANT EACH WISH, THEN EXITS.)

FLOWERS: I WISH THERE WAS A POT.
   FAIRY: YOUR WISH IS GRANTED.
    POT: I WISH THERE WAS A TABLE.
   FAIRY: YOUR WISH IS GRANTED.
  TABLE: I WISH THERE WAS A CHAIR.
   FAIRY: YOUR WISH IS GRANTED.
  CHAIR: I WISH THERE WAS A GIRL.
   FAIRY: YOUR WISH IS GRANTED.
   GIRL: I WISH THERE WAS A DISH.
   FAIRY: YOUR WISH IS GRANTED.
   DISH: I WISH THERE WAS A FISH.
   FAIRY: YOUR FISH IS GRANTED.
   GIRL: HOW DELICIOUS A FISH DISH IS.
   FISH: I DON'T LIKE IT.
           STOP THE SHOW.
           I WISH THAT EVERYTHING WOULD GO.
   FAIRY: YOUR WISH IS GRANTED.
   DISH: GOODBYE. (EXIT)
   GIRL: GOODBYE. (EXIT)
  CHAIR: GOODBYE. (EXIT)
  TABLE: GOODBYE. (EXIT)
    POT: GOODBYE. (EXIT)
FLOWERS: GOODBYE. (EXIT)
   FAIRY: GOODBYE. (STARTS TO EXIT)
   FISH: WAIT! MAY I HAVE ONE MORE WISH?
   FAIRY: YES.
   FISH: I WISH THERE WAS WATER.
   FAIRY: YOUR WISH IS GRANTED.
  WATER: SQUISH, SQUISH, SQUISH, SQUISH,
           SQUISH, SQUISH, SQUISH.
   FISH: SWISH, SWISH, SWISH, SWISH,
           SWISH, SWISH, SWISH.
  WATER: MY WISH IS THERE BE MORE FISHES.
   FAIRY: I'M TIRED OF RUNNING IN AND OUT TODAY.
           I WISH IT WAS THE END OF THIS PLAY.
FLOWERS: YOUR WISH IS GRANTED.
    POT: YOUR WISH IS GRANTED.
  TABLE: YOUR WISH IS GRANTED.
  CHAIR: YOUR WISH IS GRANTED.
   GIRL: YOUR WISH IS GRANTED.
   DISH: YOUR WISH IS GRANTED.
   FISH: YOUR WISH IS GRANTED.
  WATER: YOUR WISH IS GRANTED.

(ALL BOW AND EXIT.)

I THINK OF YOU EVERYTIME I THINK OF YOU EVERYTIME I THINK OF YOU EVERYTIME I THINK OF YOU EVERYTIME I THINK OF YOU EVERYTIME

I THINK OF YOU EVERYTIME I THINK OF YOU EVERYTIME

I AM WHAT I AM WHAT I AM WHAT I AM WHAT I AM

WHAT IS MINE IS YOURS AND WHAT IS YOURS IS MINE AND WHAT IS YOURS AND WHAT IS MINE AND WHAT IS YOURS IS MINE AND WHAT IS

ANDROUNDANDROUND ANDROUND ANDROUND

WHAT I AM WHAT I AM WHAT I AM WHAT I AM WHAT I AM WHAT

I THINK OF YOU EVERYTIME I THINK OF YOU EVERYTIME I THINK OF YOU EVERYTIME I THINK OF YOU EVE

I AM WHAT I AM WHAT I AM WHAT I AM WHAT I AM

I THINK OF YOU EVERYTIME I THINK OF YOU EVERYTIME I THINK OF YOU EVERYTIME I THINK OF YOU EVERYTIME I THINK OF YOU EVERYTIME I THINK OF YOU EVERYTIME I THINK OF YOU EVERYTIME I THINK OF YOU

THERE LIES AN OLD DOG BY THE STOVE NAMED DEAR LIZA NOLD OG BY THE STOVE NAMED ERE LIESA NOLDO GBYT HE STOVE NAMED THERE LIES AN OLD DOG BY THE STOVE NAMED

ENDLESS TAIL #1

ENDLESS TAIL #2

ENDLESS TAIL #3

BEFORE ME PEACEFUL
BESIDE ME PEACEFUL
BEHIND ME PEACEFUL
ABOVE ME PEACEFUL
BELOW ME PEACEFUL
ALL AROUND ME PEACEFUL

ME PEACEFUL

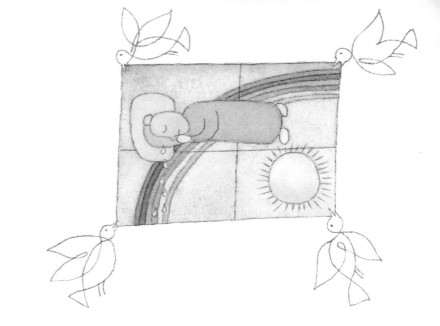

CIRCULAR SONG

OW SORR
OW PILL
OW WIND
OW RAINB

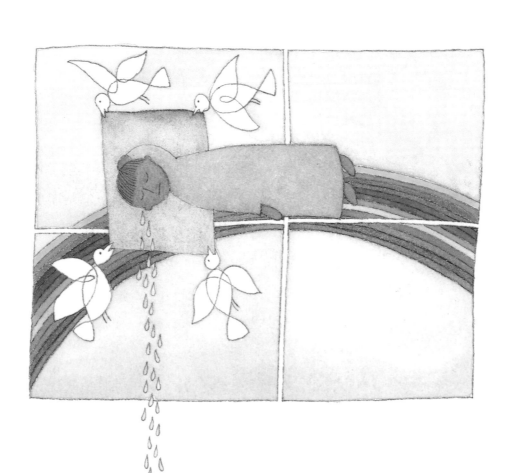

ONCE IN CHINA, A MAN GAVE AN ARTIST MONEY
TO MAKE A PAINTING OF A FISH.
THE MAN WAITED SEVERAL YEARS
AND WHENEVER HE SAW THE ARTIST
HE ASKED FOR THE PAINTING.
AFTER WAITING SEVERAL MORE YEARS
THE MAN GREW ANGRY. HE WENT TO THE ARTIST'S HOUSE
AND DEMANDED THE PAINTING.
THE ARTIST TOOK A PIECE OF PAPER
DIPPED HER BRUSH IN PAINT
AND WITH EASE DASHED OFF THE MOST BEAUTIFUL PAINTING OF A FISH.
THE MAN WAS ASTONISHED.
''IF IT WAS SO SIMPLE,'' HE SAID, ''WHY DIDN'T YOU DO IT SOONER?''
IN REPLY THE ARTIST SLID OPEN A DOOR.
THOUSANDS OF PAINTINGS OF FISH FELL OUT.

I'VE BEEN THINKING
ABOUT A VERY LITTLE MOUNTAIN
COVERED ALL OVER WITH VERY LITTLE FLOWERS
AND ON TOP
A VERY LITTLE HOUSE WITH VERY LITTLE WINDOWS
AND IF YOU LOOK INTO ONE OF THE VERY LITTLE WINDOWS
OF THIS VERY LITTLE HOUSE
YOU WILL SEE A VERY LITTLE GIRL
SITTING ON A VERY LITTLE CHAIR
NEXT TO A VERY LITTLE TABLE.
AND DO YOU KNOW WHAT IS ON THE VERY LITTLE TABLE?
A VERY LITTLE BIRTHDAY CAKE WITH VERY LITTLE CANDLES.
AND DO YOU KNOW WHAT THE LITTLE GIRL IS DOING?
SHE IS BLOWING OUT THE CANDLES
BECAUSE IT IS HER BIRTHDAY.
BUT SHE HAS TO BE VERY VERY CAREFUL
BECAUSE IT HAS TO BE A VERY LITTLE BLOW.

PETE AND REPETE WERE SITTING ON A FENCE.

PETE FELL OFF. WHO WAS LEFT?

REPETE.

PETE AND REPETE WERE SITTING ON A FENCE.

PETE FELL OFF. WHO WAS LEFT?

REPETE.

BULLETIN

SHOTT SHOT AT NOTT. BUT SHOTT'S SHOT DID NOT SHOOT NOTT.
NOTT NOT WANTING TO BE SHOT QUICKLY SHOT AT SHOTT'S SHOT.
NOTT'S SHOT SHOT SHOTT'S SHOT. LUCKILY NOT NOTT NOR SHOTT WAS SHOT.

 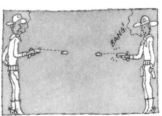 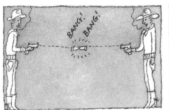 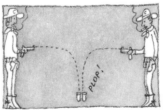

I
WANT
A
SANDWICH
WITH
SOME
HAM
AND
SOME
CHEESE
AND
SOME
BUTTER
AND
SOME
MUSTARD
AND
SOME
SALT
AND
SOME
PEPPER
AND
SOME
TOMATO
AND
SOME
LETTUCE
AND
SOME
MAYONNAISE
AND
SOME
KETCHUP
AND
SOME
RELISH
AND
YES
SOME
BREAD

I WANT A CHOCOLATE COVERED CHERRY
AND A CHOCOLATE COVERED EASTER EGG
AND A CHOCOLATE COVERED VALENTINE
AND A CHOCOLATE COVERED ICE CREAM CONE
AND A CHOCOLATE COVERED BIRTHDAY CAKE
AND A CHOCOLATE COVERED CHRISTMAS TREE
AND A CHOCOLATE COVERED SNOWMAN
AND A CHOCOLATE COVERED BICYCLE
AND SOME CHOCOLATE COVERED SPAGHETTI.

I WANT A SMALL PIECE OF STRING WITH AN ANT ON IT CARRYING A SMALL PIECE OF STRING WITH A WORM ON IT CARRYING A SMALL PIECE OF STRING WITH A DOG ON IT CARRYING A SMALL PIECE OF STRING WITH A BIRD ON IT CARRYING A SMALL PIECE OF STRING WITH A CAT ON IT CARRYING A SMALL PIECE OF STRING WITH A COW ON IT CARRYING A SMALL PIECE OF STRING WITH A HORSE ON IT CARRYING A SMALL PIECE OF STRING WITH A RHINOCEROS ON IT CARRYING A SMALL PIECE OF STRING WITH AN ELEPHANT ON IT CARRYING A SMALL PIECE OF STRING WITH A DINOSAUR ON IT CARRYING A SMALL PIECE OF STRING WITH A SMALL PIECE OF STRING ON IT.

SNORE SNORE HE SAID

RING-RING IT SAID

YAWN YAWN HE SAID

UP UP SHE SAID

YES YES HE SAID

TWEET TWEET THEY SAID

COME COME SHE SAID

SOON SOON HE SAID

NOW NOW SHE SAID

GR GR HE SAID

GR GR SHE SAID

GR GR HE SAID

WOW
MOM

TELL ME A STORY, MY SUN.

IT WAS A DARK AND STORMY NIGHT. WE WERE

MY SISTER'S MOTHER'S HUSBAND'S FATHER'S GRANDCHILD IS ME

SAVING TIME AND MONEY

A PLAY

A: LET'S BUILD A NEW HOUSE.

B: LET'S BUILD THE NEW HOUSE OUT OF THE OLD HOUSE.

C: LET'S LIVE IN THE OLD HOUSE UNTIL THE NEW HOUSE IS FINISHED.

A MAN WAS LOCKED IN HIS HOUSE AND COULDN'T GET OUT.

BUT HE KNEW HE WOULD.

HE HIT THE WOOD UNTIL HIS HANDS WERE SORE.

HE SAWED THE WOOD IN HALF.

TWO HALVES MAKE A WHOLE.

HE SHOUTED THROUGH THE HOLE UNTIL HIS VOICE WAS HOARSE.

HE JUMPED ON THE HORSE, RODE THROUGH THE WOULD AND GOT HOME SAFELY.

GEORGE WASHINGTON SLEPT HERE

BENJAMIN FRANKLIN WORKED HERE

WALT WHITMAN WROTE "LEAVES OF GRASS" HERE

QUEEN MARY HAD TEA AND CRUMPETS HERE

ABRAHAM LINCOLN DIED HERE

LONGFELLOW WAS BORN HERE

ISADORA DUNCAN DANCED HERE

MY COUNTRY 'TIS OF THEE" WAS COMPOSED HERE

PEANUT BUTTER WAS INVENTED HERE

ST. VALENTINE WAS FIRST KISSED HERE

GHOST TOWN

PART MAN PART GOAT PART FISH PART BIRD PART SNAKE PART BUG

PART CAR PART BOAT PART PLANE PART HOUSE

PART TREE PART CLOUD PART SUN PART WATER PART MOUNTAIN

A GREEN SPY WAS FOLLOWING A BLUE SPY

FOLLOWED BY A NIGHT SKY

FOLLOWED BY A FAT LIE

FOLLOWED BY A CHERRY PIE

FOLLOWED BY A STRIPED TIE

FOLLOWED BY A BLACK EYE

FOLLOWED BY A BUTTERFLY

FOLLOWED BY A DAY IN JULY

FOLLOWED BY A MAGPIE

FOLLOWED BY A DEEP SIGH

FOLLOWED BY A BYE-BYE

FOLLOWED BY A GOOD CRY

FOLLOWED BY A BLUE SPY

TEA PARTY
A PLAY

MRS. HAGGARTY: I FEEL LIKE A CUP OF TEA.
  LADY AGATHA: FUNNY, YOU DON'T LOOK LIKE ONE.
MRS. HAGGARTY: WHAT I MEANT WAS, WOULD YOU JOIN ME IN A CUP OF TEA?
  LADY AGATHA: WILL WE BOTH FIT?
MRS. HAGGARTY: NO. SILLY. I HAVE TWO CUPS. HERE. NOW. SUGAR, CREAM OR LEMON?
  LADY AGATHA: PLEASE.
MRS. HAGGARTY: ONE LUMP OR TWO?
  LADY AGATHA: SEVEN. WHAT HAND DO YOU USE TO STIR YOUR TEA WITH?
MRS. HAGGARTY: MY RIGHT.
  LADY AGATHA: DIRTY THING! USE YOUR SPOON.

TWO GENTLEMEN
A PLAY OF MANNERS

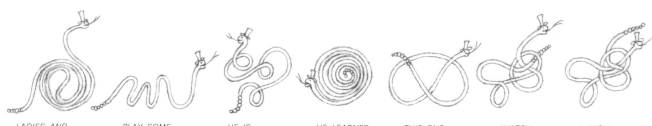

LADIES AND
GENTLEMEN!
OLD SNAKE IS
GOING TO DANCE!

PLAY SOME
SNAKE MUSIC
PLEASE.

HE IS
STRETCHING
AND WARMING
HIMSELF UP

HE LEARNED
THIS WHEN
HE WAS
VERY LITTLE

THIS ONE
IS CALLED
THE PRETZEL.

WATCH
THIS
ONE.

I WISH
I COULD DO THAT.

THIS ONE
IS CALLED
THE BUTTERFLY....

THE DOUBLE HEART....

THE SWAN....

I WOULD
BE TIRED
BY NOW.

I'LL BET
HE CAN
DANCE
ANYTHING.

HE IS SLOWING DOWN.

SLEEP WELL.
OLD SNAKE.

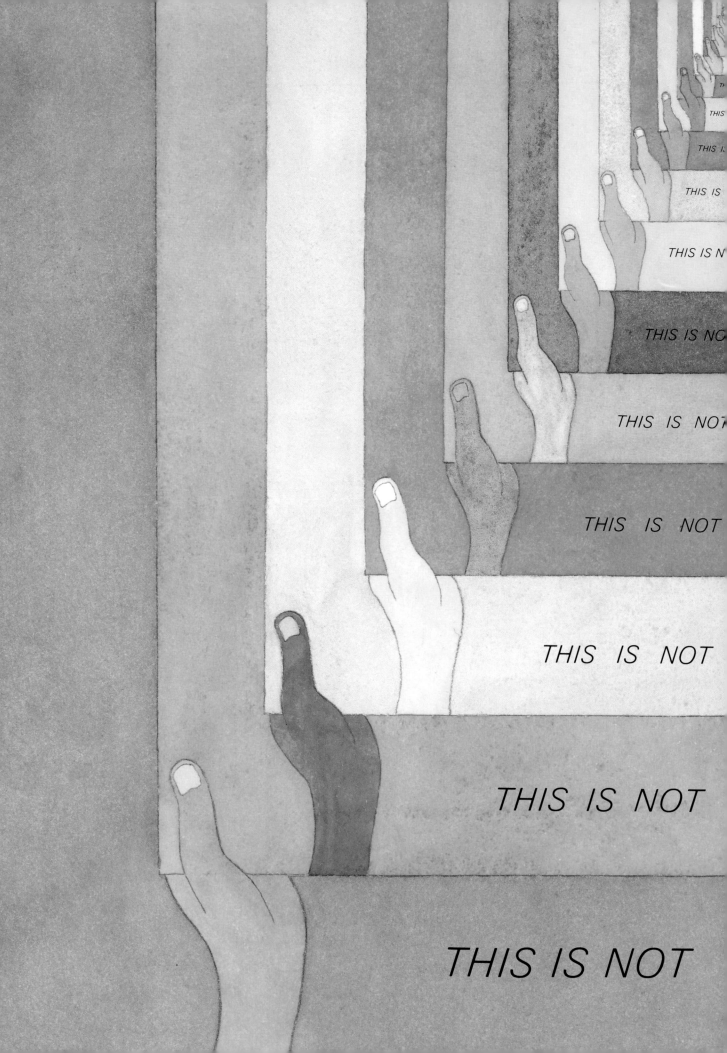

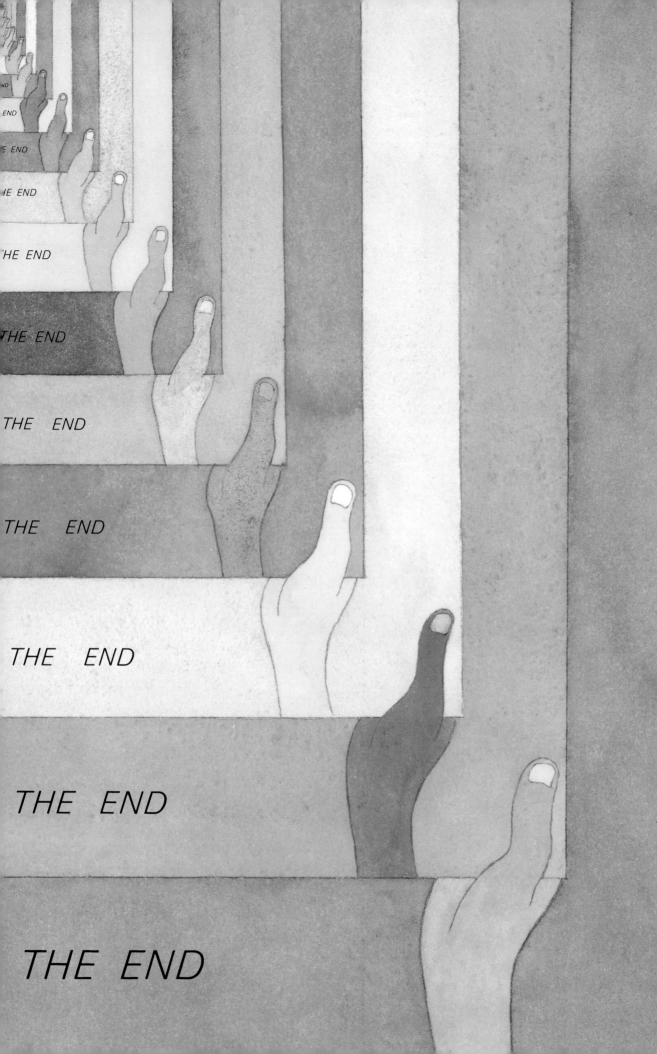